no Lexile

CHARLIE-BOB'S FAN

HARCOURT BRACE JOVANOVICH · NEW YORK AND LONDON

W. B. PARK

Charlie-Bob's Fan

Printed in the United States of America

LIBRARY OF CONGRESS CATALOGING IN PUBLICATION DATA
Park, W   B
Charlie-Bob's fan.
SUMMARY: A dog who tries everything he can
think of to turn on a fan on a hot day is outdone
by a cat who accidentally trips the switch.
[1. Fans (Machinery) — Fiction.
2. Dogs — Fiction.   3. Cats — Fiction.
4. Stories without words]   I. Title.
PZ7.P22145Ch   [E]   80-25166
ISBN 0-15-216221-6

First edition

B C D E

For Evie

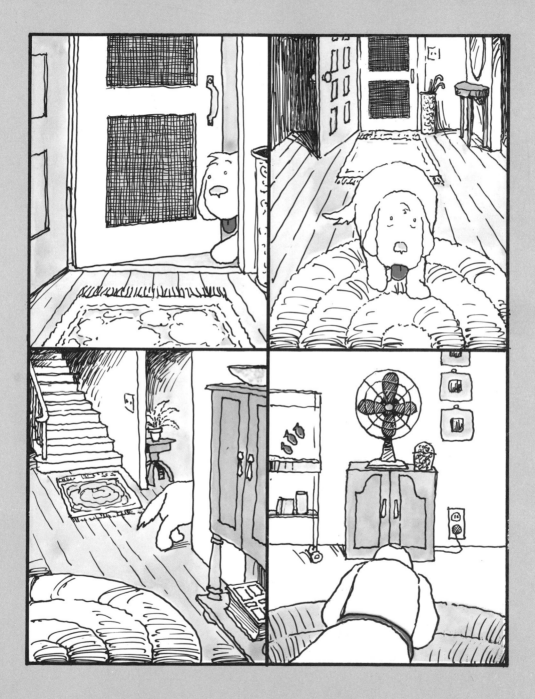

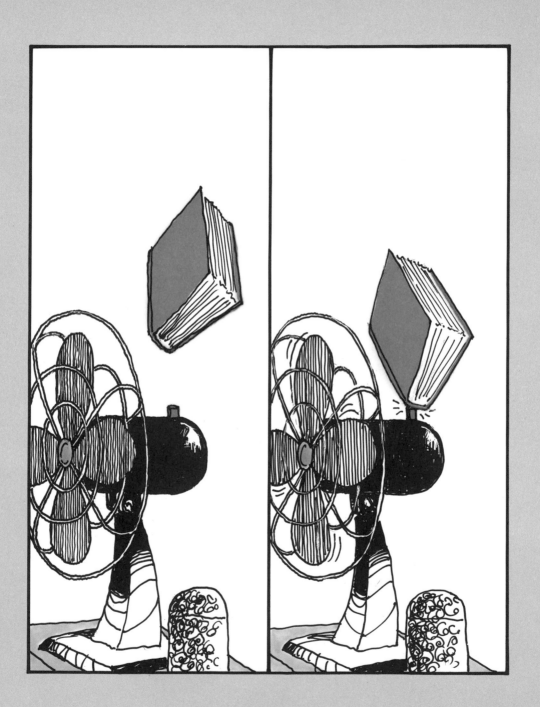

W. B. PARK was born in Sanford, Florida, and attended the University of Florida and the School of Visual Arts in New York City. He now runs a successful studio that produces advertising and commercial art, and his illustrations have appeared in many national magazines and newspapers, including *The New York Times, Smithsonian,* and *Sports Illustrated.* In addition, Mr. Park is the author and illustrator of two books for children, *The Pig in the Floppy Black Hat* and *Jonathan's Friends,* and lives in Florida with his wife, their three children, a bulldog, and a cat named (by his youngest daughter) Charlotte Web.